KID
NORMAL
AND THE
LOUDEST LIBRARY

GREG JAMES & CHRIS SMITH

ILLUSTRATED BY
ERICA SALCEDO

BLOOMSBURY
CHILDREN'S BOOKS
LONDON OXFORD NEW YORK NEW DELHI SYDNEY

Meet the
Super Zeroes

The youngest team of superheroes
ever to be accepted into the Heroes' Alliance!

NELLIE LEE
a.k.a. Rain Shadow

CAPABILITY:
Meteorological
Manipulation
(Storm control)

MARY PERKINS
a.k.a. Mary Canary

CAPABILITY:
Terrain Circumvention
(Flying, with or without
umbrella. But she prefers
with. Wouldn't you?)

If you're new to the world of Kid Normal,
this book is dedicated to YOU. Hello!

BLOOMSBURY CHILDREN'S BOOKS
Bloomsbury Publishing Plc
50 Bedford Square, London WC1B 3DP, UK

BLOOMSBURY, BLOOMSBURY CHILDREN'S BOOKS and the Diana logo
are trademarks of Bloomsbury Publishing Plc

First published in Great Britain in 2020 by Bloomsbury Publishing Plc

ISBN: 978-1-5266-1965-5

2 4 6 8 10 9 7 5 3 1

Typeset by Janene Spencer

Printed and bound in Great Britain by CPI Group (UK) Ltd,
Croydon CR0 4YY

MIX
Paper from
responsible sources
FSC® C020471

To find out more about our authors and books visit www.bloomsbury.com
and sign up for our newsletters

1

The First Mission

HALO ALERT. ALL UNITS RESPOND, read the green letters on the screen.

Murph Cooper looked up at his four friends and raised an adventurous eyebrow. They'd only officially been superheroes since 3.26 p.m. that afternoon – less than five hours ago – and they were already about to accept their first proper mission. It was kind of a big moment.

Murph looked back down at the phone-like device in his hand – the HALO or Heroes' Alliance Locator Unit. Only that afternoon it had been handed to him by the stern and impressive-haired leader of the Alliance, Miss Flint. As leader of the Super Zeroes, this device would be their way of tracking and contacting him. 'We'll call you,' Miss Flint had told him. He just hadn't quite expected it to happen that very evening.

'Go on then, answer it!' prompted Billy, one finger ballooning with excitement.

Murph smiled to himself as he contemplated Billy's unpredictable Capability, which was to inflate parts of his body or other nearby objects. Billy's Cape – as they were nicknamed in the world of Heroes – wasn't always completely under his control. But his smile sank beneath the surface once again as he realised he was about to speak to a secret organisation of superheroes. His brain still hadn't quite processed it.

You know those times when you shut your eyes in the hope it shuts your ears so you can concentrate? Murph briefly did that, thinking back to the vow he and his friends had recited earlier that day when they had become the youngest ever members of the Heroes' Alliance:

I promise to save without glory,
To help without thanks
And to fight without fear.
I promise to keep our secrets,
Uphold our vow
And learn what it means
To be a true Hero.

It had all sounded very exciting, but to be honest he'd assumed there would be a couple of weeks' grace to let the news sink in. He'd even vaguely imagined that some kind of pack might arrive in the post with an instruction book, membership card and possibly even a badge. But there was no manual, no YouTube tutorials. Nothing.

I guess it's one of those jobs you learn by doing them, thought Murph to himself decisively, opening his eyes (and ears) and lifting the handset to his mouth.

'Super Zeroes receiving!' he said firmly. 'Kid Normal active.'

Choosing 'Kid Normal' as his codename when they had joined the Alliance had been easy. It was the nickname some of the other kids in his class had given him after he'd accidentally been enrolled in The School – a secret facility where people with Capes were educated and trained. It had started off as a cruel joke because he was the only one there with no powers at all. Now he wore it as a badge of pride.

'Mary Canary active,' chimed in his best friend Mary, her yellow raincoat catching the reflections of the street light above them.

Billy added his own Hero name: 'Balloon Boy active.' He waggled a hand as if to add, 'Finger now under control,' although Murph couldn't help noticing that one of his ears had now inflated slightly.

'Equana active!' chimed in Hilda, and suddenly Murph's smile returned, his apprehensions turning to excitement. He knew that freckled, curly-haired Hilda had dreamed of this moment ever since she'd first discovered her rather unusual Cape – the ability to produce two tiny white horses from nowhere.

A soft voice completed the list as Nellie lifted a strand of green-tipped hair from her face and piped up, 'Rain Shadow active.'

Murph caught Mary's eye and she mirrored his smile. He gave one more look around the faces of his other friends, glowing softly in the green screenlight, all of them tense with anticipation.

'**Alliance calling**,' said a calm voice from the phone.

Murph did one of those nervous throat-clears that you do even when you don't need to clear your throat. We bet you just did one too. This was it.

'**Attention, Super Zeroes. Please proceed as directed to the library at The School. An operative will meet you there who requires assistance on a seek-and-apprehend mission. They will provide further information. Alliance out.**'

The HALO screen abruptly flickered into darkness. Murph and his four friends looked at each other, excitement dawning on their faces like the first sunrise of the school holidays.

'Come on then! What are you waiting for?' prompted Hilda, quivering with anticipation like a racehorse at the start line.

Wordlessly, Murph nodded, and the five Super Zeroes turned and dashed off into the gathering twilight.

2

Mr Flash's Hobby

'**H**OLD ON A SPUD-MASHING MINUTE, WHERE DO YOU BUNCH OF RIDICULOUS CHRYSANTHEMUMS THINK YOU'RE GALLOPING OFF TO?' The voice, car-horn loud and dripping with dislike, boomed into their backs like a gust of wind on a coastal walk. It stopped the five friends in their tracks as they pelted down the hallway towards the library. Murph knew before he turned around who he was going to see. Only one teacher could stuff one single sentence with such a large amount of contempt.

Mr Flash had stepped into the corridor behind them and was standing, hands on hips, in the

internationally recognised teacher stance that means, 'What on earth do you think you're doing here?'

'WHAT ON EARTH DO YOU THINK YOU'RE DOING HERE?' bellowed their CT teacher, his large ginger moustache flapping like a flag in a typhoon. Mr Flash was in charge of Capability Training lessons at The School, and made no secret of the fact that he favoured the students with more traditional powers like super-strength or -speed. Producing tiny horses, ballooning yourself or flying with the aid of an umbrella did not impress him – in fact he considered Murph and his friends nothing but a bunch of wimps – or 'maggots' as he often referred to them.

'SCHOOL'S CLOSED!' Mr Flash went on, still at Beaufort scale force-twelve volume. 'We're trying to regroup after Nektar's attack!' His frown deepened as he said this, and Murph knew why.

Up until the previous evening, Mr Flash had

been mind-controlled by an evil half-man, half-wasp. Nektar had attacked The School, enslaving some staff and pupils and taking the rest prisoner. It was Murph and his friends who had saved the day – and Mr Flash had been less than pleased that it was these 'maggots' from the bottom of his class who had rescued him. Murph had been hoping to keep the Super Zeroes out of his way for as long as possible, but here they were – trapped. Caught out of bounds. Mr Flash had a glint in his eye that said 'Gotcha'. It's hard to make a glint say 'Gotcha' but somehow he was managing it.

'Charging about school like a herd of rampagin' pheasants!' complained Mr Flash glintingly. 'You're in trouble this time, you bunch of macerated prunes.'

Murph knew that what he was about to say would make the teacher even more furious, but he had to do it anyway. Clenching up his face like a nervous bomb-disposal expert about to cut the red wire, he blurted out, 'We're here on Alliance business, Mr Flash.'

For a moment the corridor was silent except for the distant hum of a Hoover. Then Mr Flash hit them with a blast so savage that Nellie curled herself up like a prawn and Mary instinctively grabbed her eyebrows in fear they might be blown away like deckchairs in a hurricane.

'ALLIANCE ... BUSINESS?' the teacher bawled at them. Murph actually got a glimpse of his tonsils frantically clanging together like castanets as the hot air of his fury swept over them. But Kid Normal held his nerve.

'Yes, Alliance business,' he confirmed confidently.

The teacher's shoulders slumped. He was beaten. 'Go on then,' he said, looking as crestfallen as a punnet of dropped cress. ''Op it and let me get back to my embroidery.'

'Embroidery?' questioned Billy.

'WEIGHTLIFTING, I SAID!' screamed Mr Flash, going the same shade of deep red as a sunburned aubergine. **'EMBROIDERY, PAH! I'LL POPPIN' WELL EMBROIDER YOU IN A MINUTE!** Alliance business? You bunch of pathetic persimmons? Gor, I dunno. Makes me weep, it does. Weep tears of pure, molten regret.'

'That's very poetic, Mr Flash,' said Hilda encouragingly.

'Shut your tram 'ole,' scathed Mr Flash. 'Go on, get out of it.' He turned away and pushed through a set of grey double doors, muttering something about the decline of civilisation as we know it.

'Right,' said Mary brightly. 'Library?'

'Library,' Murph confirmed, following her.

3

The Fletch-Mobile

When Murph pushed open the doors to the school library, he wasn't entirely sure what he expected to see. He thought back over the message from the Alliance ...

'An operative will meet you there who requires assistance on a seek-and-apprehend mission ...'

What would this operative look like? Although Murph knew that members of the Alliance didn't wear costumes like the Heroes of the Golden Age, he couldn't help imagining a large, muscle-bound figure in a body-hugging outfit complete with mask and ... yes, gloves. Definitely gloves. Once inside, he vainly scanned the large, shelf-lined room for such a character.

'Looking for something, Mr Cooper?' came a voice from a shadowy corner away to their right. Murph did a comedy jump like a startled fawn before turning to see the librarian, Mrs Fletcher, sitting primly behind her desk sipping from a cup of tea.

In some ways, Mrs Fletcher was a fairly normal school librarian. In other ways, she was not. Let's have a look at them in the time-honoured list format, shall we?

Ways in which Mrs Fletcher was a fairly normal school librarian:

1. Loved books.
2. Worked in a library.
3. Had scanner which made a beeping noise when you took out a book.
4. Sat behind a desk.
5. Desk (see point 4) was inside a library (see point 2).

Ways in which Mrs Fletcher was not a fairly normal librarian:

1. Head turned into huge foghorn when she got angry.

'Oh, good evening, Mrs Fletcher,' replied Murph in measured tones. His ears still twinged with the memory of the last time he'd witnessed her foghorn transformation. 'Sorry to disturb you, but we got a message from the Alliance.'

'Something about a seek-and-apprehend mission?' added Hilda. 'It sounded kind of urgent.'

'We were told to meet ... an operative here?' Murph cast his eyes around once again in case he'd somehow missed a hulking be-gloved Hero amongst the books.

'Oh, really?' said Mrs Fletcher in disappointed tones, taking off her glasses and letting them dangle around her neck on their chain. 'The Alliance has sent you?' She tutted. 'I knew they weren't taking this seriously enough.'

Murph bristled slightly at this. After all, they had just saved the entire school. 'I'm sure we can help you with whatever the problem is here,' he told Mrs Fletcher.

'Oh, the problem isn't here,' she told him. 'No, no, no. It's in the library.'

'Right,' Murph replied, drawing the word out to give him a bit of thinking time. 'The library.' He was starting to think that the stress of the last couple of days might have affected Mrs Fletcher's state of mind a little.

Mrs Fletcher leaned forward across her desk. 'It's Margaret, you see,' she breathed dramatically. 'She's missing. From the library!'

Murph looked around at the neat shelves of books, wondering what on earth Mrs Fletcher could be talking about and why she kept talking about 'the library' as if it was a different place when they were, without doubt, all currently in a library.

'She's missing from ... the library,' he said calmly. 'I see.'

'Don't talk to me like I'm mad, young Mr Cooper,' said the librarian sternly. 'I'm not talking about this library, obviously. I'm talking about the main library, in the town.'

'What's going on at the main library?' asked Mary.

'I just told you!' replied Mrs Fletcher shrilly. **'My friend Margaret's gone missing!** Honestly, I thought you were supposed to be Heroes! Can't you take in the simplest information? Margaret, who runs the town library, has gone missing! I've been trying to call her all day! How many times do you need to have your mission explained to you?'

She was growing more and more agitated, and Murph was seriously worried she might be about to go full foghorn on them. 'Sorry, Mrs Fletcher,' he told her placatingly. 'We're new to all this.'

He was fighting an undeniable sense of disappointment, and glancing at his friends' faces he guessed they felt the same way. He'd been hoping for something a little more thrilling for their first mission. Say, an ocean expedition to track down

19

the Great Rodolpho, the most feared dolphin-based villain the high seas had ever seen. The prospect of a search for a missing librarian – who may just have mislaid her phone – had rather taken the wind out of his sails.

'Maybe Margaret's just … lost her phone or something?' said Hilda, echoing Murph's thoughts.

'You sound exactly like that person I spoke to at the Alliance!' said Mrs Fletcher crossly. 'But as I tried to explain to them, she isn't even picking up the main enquiry line! And let me tell you, young lady, that a good librarian never deserts their post! **Mark my words, something is wrong!'**

Murph was now convinced that the Heroes' Alliance had given them a mission that was the superhero equivalent of ten-pin bowling with the barriers up. No high-octane, swashbuckling capers. No terrifying dolphin-based baddies. Just a trip to the library to track down someone who had – in all probability – got a bit carried away digitising the catalogue and forgotten to pick up the phone.

Buckling of swashes would have to wait for another day, he decided. At least it would be an easy win. 'Super Zeroes ready and willing to help, Mrs Fletcher,' he told the librarian. 'Let's go and find Margaret.'

'About time!' she replied, getting up from behind her desk. 'There may not be a moment to lose. Come along! We'll take my car.'

Pausing only to grab her tea from the desk, she led them out of the room.

'Maybe she's got, like, a really cool Hero car or something,' said Hilda excitedly, trotting along beside Murph as they followed the librarian through The School. 'Maybe one that can fly, like the *Banshee*!'

Only the previous day they had been battling robot wasps in mid-air during an adventure in the jet-powered car flown by legendary Hero, the Blue

Phantom, and the excitement was still fresh in their minds.

'Why not share some of that excitement by grabbing yourself a copy of the first *Kid Normal* book from all good booksellers or your local library?' said a passing ant, but nobody except you could hear it.

'I am rather surprised they sent you five to help me,' said Mrs Fletcher as she turned a corner and led them down a long hallway that ran along the back of The School. 'I would have thought they would have sent some proper ... that is, properly *experienced* operatives along. Who knows what horrors we may encounter?'

'Overdue library books?' whispered Billy to Murph. 'Her worst nightmare.' Murph grinned at him.

'Here we are,' said Mrs Fletcher, leading them out of a set of side doors to the area where The School staff parked their cars.

'The critically acclaimed sequel, *Kid Normal and the Rogue Heroes*, and the thrilling third book, *Kid Normal and the Shadow Machine*, are also available,' shouted the ant at the top of its voice just before the doors closed. 'And the eagerly awaited final instalment of the series, *Kid Normal and the Final Five*, is out soon!' Once again nobody but you heard the ant, which was lucky because its aggressive sales pitch was becoming slightly embarrassing and had no place in this story.

There were two vehicles in the staff car park. One was a large, gleaming SUV with tinted windows and fat black tyres. The other was a small, shoe-shaped car painted the kind of greenish brown colour that cat owners sometimes find spattered on their kitchen floor at 6 a.m.

Which car do you think belonged to Mrs Fletcher? Yeah, it's the shoe.

'Good evening, Mrs Fletcher! Good evening, fledgling Heroes!'

said a deep, authoritative voice behind them. The School's head teacher, Mr Souperman, had come through the doors, stepping on the sales ant in the process. He was making his way to the SUV, beeping it open as he walked. 'What are you all doing crowding round my large automobile?'

Murph and the rest of the Zeroes had wishfully thought that the large SUV was Mrs Fletcher's and began to back away casually, trying to hide their disappointment.

'Official Alliance business, sir!' said Murph cheerily as he turned and walked towards the shoe car.

'Some backup would be rather

welcome, actually,' added Mrs Fletcher, fumbling with her car keys. 'Missing person! We could use some muscle on this one.'

'Ah, indeed,' said Mr Souperman. 'I checked the Alliance mission log before I left. Your friend Charlotte is missing?'

'Margaret!'

'Just so. Precisely.'

'So, will you help?'

'Yes, yes, yes,' soothed Mr Souperman. **'But no.** No. I am not, as they say, present and/ or correct tonight.' The head had a habit of muddling his words when under pressure. 'I would if I could,' he went on, 'and would that I could. But I would not. Could not, that is to say.'

'You won't?'

'Exactly!' He beamed at them. 'This merry band of gentlemen and ladies will be more than up to the task, I'm sure, Mrs Fletcher. It's on the low priority list, after all.'

'Low priority?' said the librarian indignantly.

'Just so! Excellent, excellent.' The head climbed into his driving seat. 'No, no, no, you don't want me cluttering the place up. It's a perfect first mission for these new recruits. Low priority … low risk! After all, mission is as mission does. No, wait. That's not what I mean. 'Every mission … is worth two in the bush.' That is to say …' He closed his door and began to reverse out of his parking space, winding his window down to finish his attempt at wise words. **'Mission … ah, mission you already!'** With that, he gunned his engine and roared away, raising a hand casually out of the window in farewell.

'Mission you already?' smiled Mary to Murph. 'That is a new low, even for him.'

'Come on, get in, get in,' urged Mrs Fletcher. She had climbed into the cat-sick-coloured car and was beckoning them. 'Low priority indeed! Anything could have happened to Margaret for all they know. She could be ... I don't know, being held prisoner or anything! And the rush-hour traffic is a nightmare. Let's get moving.'

'Maybe this is some kind of clever camouflage car, and when she presses a button it turns into, like, a tank or something,' said Hilda hopefully as she clambered into the narrow back seat, sandwiching herself between an already-squashed Murph, Nellie and Billy.

'Ready?' said Mrs Fletcher as Mary closed the passenger door and fastened her seatbelt. The librarian reached out for a large button on the dashboard. It was one of those buttons that had a guard over it to avoid accidental detonation.

'See! This is it!' enthused Hilda. 'Hold on to your trousers! **Tank transformation, go go go!'**

'Tank transformation? Don't be ridiculous,' said Mrs Fletcher, as a cup holder extended underneath the button. 'I'm not saving anyone unless there's somewhere to put my tea. You youngsters have got a lot to learn!' She placed her tea neatly in the holder and started the engine.

The ant, which was not seriously injured and would go on to make a full recovery, waved weakly at them as they drove away.

4

The Loudest Library

It would be very exciting at this point to be able to write something like 'The Super Zeroes raced through the twilight streets towards their enemy, hearts thumping as the Fletch-mobile screeched around each corner.' But it didn't really happen like that, so here's a less exciting but more truthful sentence.

The Super Zeroes were driven safely through the twilight streets towards their enemy, well within the speed limit and obeying all relevant road markings and signage.

Well, it's not always like the stories, you know. Sorry.

As they drove, Murph let out a small sigh. He'd

already been down about the mission, and Mr Souperman's confirmation that it was indeed considered 'low priority' had deflated him even further. But, as he studied the back of Mrs Fletcher's head and saw the beaded wire that ran round her neck to keep her glasses poised for action in a dangling position, he realised he also felt a little rankled on her behalf. If you looked at it from her point of view, she'd had her concerns as good as dismissed by the Alliance and then been lumped with the youngest ever recruits to keep her quiet. What if there really *was* a mystery? The Heroes' Alliance clearly didn't think so ... Mr Souperman didn't think so. But, more than anyone else in the world of Heroes, Murph Cooper knew what it felt like to be underestimated and ignored. If Mrs Fletcher thought something was wrong, he decided, they would try their best to help her. That was what Heroes did. And before long, he had begun to suspect that the mission might not be as dull as any of them had expected.

It's not often you hear a library before you see it. But even before they turned into the street where the town library was located, the car began to vibrate with a **thudding, stomping** rhythm. It sounded like an entire army was marching up and down, having just taken delivery of a consignment of unnecessarily heavy boots.

Murph's scalp prickled as Mrs Fletcher's cat-sick green car pulled up not far away from the front doors. 'What in the name of Melvil Dewey is going on in there?' she asked, squinting through the windscreen. The road outside the library was thick with parked cars, and bright light streamed from the windows.

'We'll go and scope it out,' Murph told her.

She nodded in agreement. 'I'll find somewhere to park. Be careful!'

'Super Zeroes, assemble!' Murph told the others, squeezing gratefully out of the back seat. The evening had begun to shade into night as the car crept away, gravel clicking beneath its wheels. A comforting rectangle of golden light spread out from the double doors of the library, at the top of a set of well-worn concrete steps. And still the thumping and thudding reverberated through the air. Murph could actually see the bushes that lined the steps vibrating.

'OK,' he asserted ... assertively, 'Here's what we should do. First of all, we need some low-level reconnaissance to work out what's causing this noise, but only one—'

He was interrupted by Hilda darting away towards the library.

'On it!' she cried over her shoulder.

'Hilda! Be careful! You don't know what the next part of the plan is!' he called after her in a slightly weird shouty whisper.

'What is she doing?' sighed Mary. 'This isn't exactly classic teamwork, is it?' But after a moment,

Hilda came galumphing back, triumphantly clutching a piece of paper in her hand.

'The greatest Heroes work on instinct,' she panted, handing the paper to Murph. 'I saw it on the door and thought it would be a clue, so I went for it.'

'Well, good work, but let's stick together in future,' Murph warned kindly.

'Yes, SIR! Sorry, sir,' grinned Hilda, blushing but full of pride that she had done good work.

As Murph started flattening out the crumpled sheet of paper, Mrs Fletcher crossed the road towards them.

'I've never seen so many cars here so late,' she said suspiciously. 'Very fishy. What's this, then?' she added, seeing the paper.

'A clue!' beamed Hilda. 'I found it on the door.'

'Oh excellent! Good job, young lady,' she congratulated her. Hilda's beam turned into a beacon.

The Zeroes and Mrs Fletcher all peered at the piece of paper:

TOWN LIBRARY:
NEW PROGRAMME OF EVENTS

MONDAY: Shouting Club

TUESDAY: Woodpecker Display Team

WEDNESDAY: Indoor Clay
Pigeon Shooting

THURSDAY: Stamping Competition

FRIDAY: Hitting Dustbins with
Cricket Bats

SATURDAY: Pneumatic Drill
Masterclass

SUNDAY: Cow Choir

Free goody bags for everyone
attending! Come and make lots
of lovely noise!

'Oooh, I wish it was Sunday,' said Mary, reading over his shoulder. 'I love cows. And choirs.'

'It's Thursday today. What's on?' Billy wanted to know, craning across to try and see the sheet.

'Stamping competition, it says here,' said Murph.

'Sounds like it!' added Mary, wincing as a particularly ear-punishing burst of stomping washed over them.

'It's the loudest library I've ever heard of!' marvelled Hilda. 'Does your friend Margaret like loud things, Mrs Fletcher?'

Mrs Fletcher reacted as if Hilda had asked if her friend Margaret enjoyed making puppies cry. 'Loud things?' she hooted. 'Loud things? Certainly not, young lady. Never during business hours. Whatever's going on in there is not Margaret's work. There's something afoot at that library.'

'Quite literally,' said Murph.

'What?' snapped Mrs Fletcher.

'Well, you know ... stamping competition?

Feet … afoot … stamping a foot … ? Oh, forget it.'

There was an awkward silence as they waited for the memory of that joke to float off into oblivion and hopefully into the engine of a passing jumbo jet so they never had to hear it again.

Murph broke the silence.

'Right … well, I suggest we go and take a look. Let's creep up to those bushes near the door. We need to see what's going on in there, and who's behind it.'

As the gang crept closer, the thudding grew so loud that they actually put their hands over their ears. Once the six Heroes (all librarians are Heroes by default) had weaved their way through the branches, they poked their heads over the parapet to see what was going on.

The large, well-lit main space of the library was packed with people, all stamping on the wooden floor as hard as they could. Murph could actually see the books on the shelves behind them jumping and juddering with each impact. And standing on the desk conducting the proceedings was a small man in a dark suit with a perfectly smooth bald head and dark little eyes.

'And STAMP two three four, STAMP two three four,' Murph could hear him shouting in a high-pitched voice. 'That's excellent, yes, very good indeed! **And STAMP two three four, STAMP STAMP STAMP.'**

'Weirdest library activity ever,' said Billy into his ear.

'Until Sunday, anyway,' Murph reminded him, waving the schedule.

The small man now pulled a complicated-looking remote control out of his pocket and Murph saw him press a button. 'That's all for tonight, ladies and gentlemen,' he said in his squeaky voice. 'See you tomorrow for Hitting Dustbins with Cricket Bats. Same time! Thank you, excellent stamping tonight!

You can all collect your goody bag on the way out.'

'Down!' Murph shout-whispered.

The Zeroes and Mrs Fletcher quickly ducked down into the laurel bushes like those whack-a-mole games at the seaside as the library doors opened and people began to spill out and disperse.

'That was weird,' Murph heard someone say to their friend as they wandered past.

'I know,' the friend replied, 'my feet are killing me. Still, great goody bag. Ooh, look, cinema tickets! Cool! It was definitely worth it for these!'

Cars started up and drove away. As the final people left the library and trickled down the stairs, the lights were turned out and they heard the door lock.

'Did anyone see that little conductor man come out?' Murph enquired suspiciously as he led the Zeroes out of the bushes and into the now-deserted street.

'Nope, I didn't,' replied Mary.

'Definitely not,' agreed Hilda.

Billy and Nellie both shook their heads.

'Hmmm', said Murph, 'have you ever seen that man before, Mrs Fletcher?'

'Never in my life', she said firmly. 'Only Margaret takes the classes in there usually. Nothing about this adds up at all. It's horribly peculiar.' She looked nervously at the darkened library.

'I agree. Why is he still in there? And why would he be sitting in the dark?' questioned Billy. 'Sounds like a fruit loop to me.'

'Only one way to find out,' said Murph. 'Come on, Zeroes. We're going in to ask him personally. This is where the mission really starts!'

'Hang on,' said Mary suddenly. 'What if I need to fly?'

'What if you do need to fly?' asked Murph, nonplussed.

'I don't have my umbrella,' Mary explained, shaking her head.

'But Mary,' said Murph, 'you just found out you can fly without it, remember? When you rescued me from certain death? It was kind of a moment.'

'I know,' said Mary, blushing slightly and scuffing a foot on the road, 'but I still like to have an umbrella when I fly. It kind of helps me focus.'

'It's a comfort umbrella, if you ask me,' said Murph sagely to the others. 'She just feels like she needs to have it with her, but she doesn't really.'

'Oh really, is that all it is?' Mary retorted. **'You mean like you and Baby Bloon Bloon?'**

'What?' blustered Murph.

'What?' echoed Billy, Nellie, Hilda and Mrs Fletcher at the same time.

'Oh yes, his mum told me all about it,' explained Mary. 'Apparently, when Murph was little, he drew a sad face on a balloon and called it Baby Bloon Bloon, and he refused to go anywhere—'

'This isn't relevant to the mission!' shrilled

Murph desperately, his voice cracking.

'Baby Bloon Bloon?' cackled Billy.

'Please stop,' begged Murph, looking at Mary with his most pleading puppy-like expression.

'Oh, all right,' said Mary, grinning wickedly. 'I won't tell them how you used to put it in a toy pram and—'

'Umbrella!' squeaked Murph. 'Let's get you an umbrella, shall we? Umbrella for Mary immediately, please!'

'I have a spare umbrella in my boot, if you'd like to borrow it,' said Mrs Fletcher, suppressing a smile with difficulty.

'Yes please,' said Murph gratefully.

'It does have a rather sharp point on the end,' warned the librarian, walking across the road to her car and rummaging in the back, 'so do keep it away from Baby Bloon Bloon.' The others erupted into fresh giggles. Murph closed his eyes softly and puffed out his cheeks, looking not unlike a balloon with a face drawn on it himself for a moment. 'Ah, here we are,' said Mrs Fletcher, pulling a long green shape from the boot. 'It belongs to my young nephew, but I'm sure he won't mind you using it, as long as you're careful with its eyes.'

'Eyes?' said Mary, accepting the umbrella and pushing the button. It extended to reveal a green canopy decorated with a wide, smiley mouth and two large goggly eyes.

'It's a frog,' said Billy unnecessarily.

Mary, deciding it would do, furled the frog and stuck it into her belt like a sword.

'Ready for the mission now?' asked Murph desperately.

'Ready for the mission,' confirmed Mary. 'In we go!'

'In … to the creepy dark building?' said Billy uncertainly.

'Into the creepy dark building … together,' Hilda reassured him, giving his leg a comforting squeeze.

'It'll be all dark and smell of books,' whimpered Billy.

'That's libraries at night for you,' reasoned Murph. 'Come on.'

Mrs Fletcher took a final swig of tea from her mug, then joined Murph and his friends. Together, they began to move towards the darkened building.

5

Breaking and Entering

'**H**ow do you break into a library?' queried Hilda. 'Should Mary fly up to the roof with the frog-brella, come down the stairs inside and smash a window with the heaviest atlas she can find?'

'Certainly not!' said Mrs Fletcher, horrified. She rummaged in her handbag, pulling out a slim gunmetal-grey box.

'This is when it pays to be chief tea-and-biscuit supplier to the school's caretaker, who also happens to be one of the best engineers in the world. This is a little whoojamaflip Carl knocked up for me in return for a month's supply of Jaffa Cakes,' Mrs Fletcher explained. 'It can open more or less any lock, so I have access to every library in the world.'

Oh and by the way don't even bother getting us started on the 'Jaffa Cake isn't a biscuit' debate. We haven't got time and this is only supposed to be a short story.

'You could break in anywhere with that,' marvelled Billy. 'You could go into a bank, a sweet shop, soup factory ...'

'Why would you want to break into anything other than a library?' sniffed Mrs Fletcher.

'Free soup?' suggested Billy meekly.

The Zeroes readied themselves.

'Focus, everyone. Assume battle formation. Be prepared,' Murph reminded them.

As the Zeroes stiffened with anticipation, Mrs Fletcher carefully placed the grey box over the lock on the door and it began to whirr into action. There was a hum, followed by a clicking sound and a highly pleasing pop, and the door swung open abruptly.

The room contained neither the little bald man nor Margaret.

'Oh,' said Murph, 'that's an anticlimax. Keep alert, Zeroes. Eyes peeled for any clues or signs of Margaret.'

The library shelves stretched away from them into the gloom. 'Let's see what we can find,' Murph instructed them. 'There was something very suspicious about that little guy organising all the racket, and he's still lurking in here somewhere. Let's see if we can find where he went.'

The Super Zeroes fanned out and began to wander around. Murph walked down the central aisle of shelves, passing through a chequerboard of shadows on the floor as the evening moonlight spilled in through the high windows. His nose was filled with a reassuring booky smell, and he wondered what on earth he was supposed to be looking for. Nothing looked particularly out of place.

'Over here!' said Mrs Fletcher, who had naturally gravitated towards the issue desk. 'There's no sign of Margaret, but she's left her date-stamp ink lidless and she'd NEVER do that willingly.'

'Where *is* this guy?' said Murph with exasperation in his voice.

Suddenly he felt a crunch underfoot and bent down. It was a pile of chalky soil on the floor.

'Mary,' he hissed.

'Did you find something?' she asked, coming alongside him and bending down. 'Oooh, zowie! Another clue. What do you think it means?'

He shrugged, at a loss. What was soil doing in a library?

'Footprints!' realised Mary, pointing to a faint outline on the floor. Sure enough, a trail of dusty prints led away from the pile of soil. They began to follow it.

On the other side of the library, Hilda had decided to pop her horses into being to help with the search. They ran around the library floor for a moment, noses pressed to the parquet like tiny terriers, before they both turned and cantered off

towards the back wall. Murph and Mary, coming round the corner, were almost bowled over as they dashed past. 'They're on the trail too!' Murph realised. 'Follow those tiny horses!'

They followed the sound of miniature hooves, and caught up with the horses beside a large, imposing bookcase.

'The footprints stop at the bookshelf,' realised Mary, peering down. 'How is that possible?'

The horses were both pawing at the ground

and emitting tiny neighs at the foot of the bookcase.

'They picked up a scent!' said Hilda as she, Billy and Nellie approached.

'What have you found?' asked Mrs Fletcher, hurrying over from the front desk.

'We have found,' said Billy, squinting up into the gloom to read the sign on top of the large bookcase:

> Extremely boring politics books full of long speeches. No need to read ever. Go away.

'It's a secret door! Got to be!' realised Murph. 'I love a secret bookcase door. I've seen these before. **Start pulling the books!'**

'What?' asked Billy.

'One of the books is a trick book, and when you pull it forward it releases the door,' explained Murph. 'Have you never seen a secret bookcase door before?'

'You watch too many films,' said Mary, but together with the others she started pulling books towards her at random.

'These books do look really dull, to be fair,' said Billy, reading the spines. '*Great Railway Speeches of the 1850s … A Potted History of the Iron Girder … Pull This Book to Open the Secret Door … Great Victorian Hat-Wearers …*'

'What did you just say?' said Murph sharply.

'Wearers,' replied Billy.

'No, before that!'

'Great Victorian hat?'

'Before THAT!'

'Pull this book to open … Oh!' realised Billy, pulling the spine. There was a clank, and they all looked around to see what had clanked.

'What clanked?' whispered Murph.

'Not sure,' said Mary uncertainly, looking around at Billy, Nellie and Hilda. Everyone responded with shakes of the head and baffled expressions.

'I think the clank was caused by the opening of a trapdoor,' said the voice of Mrs Fletcher, sounding rather strange and echoey.

'Where are you?' said Murph, puzzled.

'Down here,' said Mrs Fletcher's voice.

Murph looked down. A large trapdoor had indeed opened up in the floor beside them, revealing a shaft leading down into the earth. Bare light bulbs were strung up here and there, and rough wooden ladders had been tied together to make what looked like a treacherous climb downwards. Hanging from the topmost ladder was Mrs Fletcher, glaring up at them disapprovingly.

'Real Heroes,' she told Murph acidly, **'always check that nobody is standing on a trapdoor before opening it.'**

'Sorry, Mrs Fletcher,' said Murph, embarrassed.

'Luckily I spent many years during my youth as a trapeze artist,' sniffed Mrs Fletcher, whom Murph

now noticed was clinging to the ladder with just one hand. 'Once you've learned circus skills, they never truly leave you. It's like riding a unicycle.'

'A secret tunnel!' gasped Hilda, peering down.

'A creepy tunnel that goes into the dark earth underneath the library,' confirmed Billy. 'I suppose this is where we go back to the car and call for backup?' he continued hopefully. 'We've surely done enough hero-ing for one week. Guys?'

'We certainly are not calling for backup!' sniffed Mrs Fletcher. 'You five *are* the backup, remember? There's clearly something very wrong here, and I intend to find out what. My friend Margaret could well be at the bottom of this tunnel. So we're going to climb down this ladder and smack some baddy bottom!' Her tartan skirt swished as, hand over hand, she began to skilfully descend.

'Best Hero catchphrase ever, bar none,' murmured Hilda to Nellie as the Super Zeroes began one by one to follow. Nellie squeaked softly in agreement.

6

The Temple of Mithras

The strange, perfectly circular tunnel led straight downwards. Murph felt giddy as he clutched on to the ladders, which swung from side to side alarmingly. The bare electric bulbs cast an unwholesome orangey glow.

'I wonder what kind of villain makes his lair underneath a library,' mused Hilda, who was climbing just below him. 'I bet he's called, like, The Bookworm or something. And he eats paper, so he's gradually stealing all the tales in the world. And so by defeating him, we're saving stories! Then maybe one day it could be made into a book and become part of a worldwide initiative to celebrate the joy of reading, or something!'

'That sounds like a rather lazy plot,' sniffed Mrs Fletcher, overhearing. 'I would hope that any authors selected for such a prestigious event had a little more imagination than that.'

Murph glanced downwards, but he could make out nothing except a glint from the librarian's glasses as they caught the light from the bulbs. His head swam as Mary stepped on to the ladder above him, causing it to swing even more wildly. He decided not to look down again, or indeed at anything apart from the rung in front of his face, so it was a slight shock when, a few moments later, his foot touched the floor. He slumped gratefully against the wall and looked around.

The bottom of the shaft had been widened out into a larger area, with rough earthen walls scarred with long, deep gouges. The soil on the floor had been trampled flat by large, rectangular footprints, which Mrs Fletcher was now examining.

'This all appears to have been dug quite

recently,' she said, rubbing a handful of soil between thumb and forefinger.

'It looks like a giant rabbit hole,' observed Billy, jumping off the lowermost ladder.

'Curiouser and curiouser,' replied Mrs Fletcher. 'And what's this?'

Murph pulled himself away from his comforting patch of wall and followed the librarian over to the far side of the hole. There, still partially covered in soil, was a stone archway, partially collapsed and tilted over to one side. The finely carved pillars were enormous – twice the height of a normal person – and set on top was a stone statue of a bull.

'This isn't just a hole,' mused Mrs Fletcher, running a hand over one of the columns, **'it's an excavation!'**

'These are Roman ruins!' added Hilda excitedly, peering through the gloom to make out details of the statue. 'This must have been down here for more than a thousand years!'

'You never know what you'll find if you go digging around in a library,' replied Murph in a whisper.

The centre of the archway had been cleared of earth, and a string of light bulbs led away down a stone passageway. As they strained their eyes to try and make out where it might lead, Mrs Fletcher abruptly held a finger up to her lips to say 'Silence' and cupped a hand to her ear to add the word 'Listen'. Murph strained his ears. There was indeed a faint sound coming down the tunnel. A **clumping** and **chinking**, punctuated by a strange **whirring** noise.

At this point, Murph realised that he hadn't had any tea and was absolutely starving. You don't often get that kind of detail in superhero stories, but we promise it's relevant to the plot and you'll find out why soon. However, there was no time for him to consider it any further, or indeed root around in his pockets for unremembered biscuits, because Mrs Fletcher continued her mime-mission-leadership by beckoning them as she ducked beneath the arch and began to pick her way along the uneven stone floor.

Hilda's eyes were so wide as she walked beside Murph that he was slightly worried they might give away their position by flying out of the front of her head with a loud popping noise. She kept gesturing at alcoves and carvings on the walls as they went, her curly hair jerking in excitement. The stone ceiling overhead was arched and beautifully constructed – Hilda was walking through her own personal ancient-historical theme park, only without the overpriced hot dogs.

Murph felt a familiar eel of anxiety pop its head out of its eel-hole and perform a couple of laps of his stomach, swimming backstroke. He was acutely conscious that this was his first mission as Lead Superhero. The Heroes' Alliance had obviously thought this would be a simple, straightforward task: track down the missing librarian. But he was now realising he had led the Super Zeroes into something far deeper and – quite possibly – much more dangerous. The anxiety eel switched to front crawl.

He kept his eyes fixed on Mrs Fletcher's back as she walked ahead, anxious to pick up any tips on what real Heroes did on missions like this. She was tiptoeing along, one hand brushing the stone wall beside them. He tried to mimic this stance, but just ended up looking like a dainty – albeit secretive – ballet dancer. As he walked gingerly along (or *pas marché*'d, for any ballet fans out there), the chinking, clumping and whirring grew louder and louder.

Mrs Fletcher held up a hand, and Murph's stomach-eel broke into an energetic burst of butterfly. They had arrived at the end of the stone passageway.

Again, this entranceway had been blocked until

recently – a second stone arch had stood here but this one had completely caved in on itself. The weathered blocks had been partially cleared away to make a small opening, but there was a large pile of tumbled rock that made a perfect hide-behind-it-and-peep area. The Super Zeroes, clustering behind Mrs Fletcher like ducklings following a crime-fighting duck, hid behind it and peeped.

If you were a fan of Roman ruins, it was quite a moment. Hilda – who was – had to hold in a gasp of pure wonder. Imagine a fan of cuteness being ushered into a large room containing exactly nine dozen fluffy puppies. Similar to that.

The collapsed arch led on to a huge room. The Zeroes could only see around half of it, but even that half was packed with statues, mosaics and gold … lots of gold. Ancient gold coins … glittering and priceless, winking in the soft light from the suspended bulbs. They lay strewn around the floor, spilling from rotted wooden chests or gathered together in rough heaps like swept leaves. Only really, really expensive leaves.

The room seemed to have been carved out of an existing cave – here and there the walls were rocky and unfinished. But elsewhere columns and arches had been built, and the floor was decorated with elaborate, multicoloured mosaics. It was – archaeological spoiler alert – the most perfectly preserved Roman temple ever discovered in the entire country. An underground shrine to the Roman god Mithras, who Hilda will be happy to tell you all about if you ever happen to meet her, as long as you promise to buy her an ice cream afterwards to say thank you.

But the person who'd discovered this hidden temple – and the wonderful historical treasures within – had no intention of telling anyone about it. He just wanted to steal all that gold. And his name… his name was Roman Goldstealer. Yes, seriously.

Villain Names: An Apology

Dear Reader,

At this point in the story, you may be thinking something along the lines of this: 'There's a villain stealing Roman gold and his name is Roman Goldstealer? Are you two idiots serious?' Now, at first sight this may look like we just thought up a name in about five seconds. But we'd like to make it clear that we've been back through the records of the Heroes' Alliance and his name was quite definitely Roman Goldstealer. There's nothing we can do about it, it's just a massive coincidence. Now can we please get on with the story? There's an exciting bit coming up, with a robot and everything. If you still have any complaints, please put them down in writing, tie them to the leg of a bird of some description and tell it to fly to the following address:

Lazy Villain Names Complaints Department

World Book Day

The World

Thank you.

Love,

Chregstopher and Griggomorph

PS Please note we are unable to return any birds. We will be keeping them, and forming them into a gigantic bird army.

From his vantage point behind the pile of tumbled stone, Murph still couldn't see what was making the strange noises that were filling the underground temple. The whirring was harsh and loud, punctuated by the clinking of metal and the occasional dull, vibrating thump, as if something heavy had slammed hard into the floor. Murph decided he had to see what they were up against. Slowly he crawled around the side of the rock pile to bring the far half of the room into view.

At the other end of the temple, the glow of the bare light bulbs was blocked by an enormous, hulking figure. It was hard to judge its height as it was bending down, but Murph guessed it was easily twice as tall as any of the Super Zeroes, with a thick chunky body and huge arms festooned with wires and tubing. At that moment it was bent over something on the ornate mosaic floor.

As Murph watched, it lifted one of those enormous arms, pulling a fistful of gold coins from a hole in the ground, and there came that same odd whirring noise. Murph felt a nudge on his arm, and turned to see that Mary had wriggled her way around to lie beside him and peep out. They were, in fact, co-peeping.

It's a robot, he mouthed to her. Unfortunately she couldn't lip-read very well.

I can't lip-read very well, she mouthed back at him.

What? Murph mouthed, also being quite bad at lip-reading.

I said, mouthed Mary, *that I can't lip-read very well. Are you trying to say 'It's a robot?' Because I'd worked that out for myself.*

Cheese and onion, mouthed Murph, who had completely misunderstood the last mouth.

What are you two mouthing to each other? mouthed Billy, poking his head in between them.

Fortunately for all of us, a new voice broke in at this point.

'Gold, ah yes! Wonderful, shiny gold!' said the voice, which was high-pitched and reedy. Not the voice you'd expect a giant robot to have, to be honest, which explains the puzzled looks the Super Zeroes immediately began exchanging.

'Finally, after all these days of digging, we have broken through to the main temple,' continued the voice. 'Our excavation is nearly complete! Put these coins in the chest with the rest. **Oooh, that rhymes!'**

The enormous figure stood up straight and began lumbering over to one side of the room, towards a large wooden crate. There was a clanking, chinking sound as it opened its metal fist, dumping the coins inside.

It is at this point that we need to remind you about that paragraph a few pages ago when we told you that Murph hadn't had any tea and was starving. Seemed totally irrelevant at the time, didn't it? Not the sort of detail you felt like you needed? Didn't add anything to the story? Well – in the nicest possible way and without meaning any offence – in your face, reader, because it's about to become super-relevant.

'Arrrrrrrrrr,' said Murph's hungry stomach, sounding like the dying breath of a pirate. Mrs Fletcher shushed him frantically, but it's very difficult – if not totally impossible – to stop your stomach growling once it's started.

'Arrrrrrrrrr,' Murph's stomach went on, as if the actor playing the dying pirate was really milking the part.

As the last breath of the tummy-pirate faded away, silence descended on the temple. Murph and Mary froze, realising that the gigantic robot had stopped moving. But then suddenly red lights began to flash on its shoulders. **'Danger,'** it intoned in a booming voice. **'Intruders.'**

'Now that's more like a scary giant-robot voice,' said Billy, quickly ducking back out of view. There was a series of clanks and thumps as the robot straightened up and turned around.

'Well, well, well, what have we here?' broke in the original voice, the thin, high-pitched one. 'A few visitors, come to see the Temple of Mithras? Don't be shy, my friends, step out and have a proper look!'

'Why has the robot got two different voices?'

complained Billy. 'That is a totally unnecessary feature.'

Murph, who thought he recognised the high, reedy voice from his earlier spying mission to the library upstairs, was about to answer him. But before he could speak, Mrs Fletcher stepped boldly out from behind the rock pile. 'It's just me,' Murph heard her say. 'There's nobody else here.'

'Oh, really?' asked the squeaky voice scornfully. 'Then who are the five children crouched down in the collapsed archway just behind you?'

'He's got X-ray vision!' wailed Hilda.

'Of course I have X-ray vision!' snapped the voice. 'That is what makes me the greatest archaeologist the world has ever seen!'

'Come on,' Murph told the others. 'No point hiding. Let's get out there and see what we're dealing with.'

'Then open up a bag of bottom-whoop!' agreed Hilda, scrambling to her feet and following him out into the temple. 'No villain is a match for the Super Zer ... oh.'

Hilda trailed off mid-sentence as she got her first proper look at their enemy and realised where the two different voices were coming from. It was quite a sight, so here's a whole paragraph describing what the Super Zeroes faced as they came out from behind the rocks and stood beside Mrs Fletcher.

The robot, now standing fully upright, was even larger than Murph had guessed. It towered towards the ceiling, casting a giant black shadow across the mosaic floor. Its head was a huge drill, and each of its arms was tipped by a pair of large metal pincers which looked more than a little dangerous. And nestled in a chair-like structure attached to the robot's broad chest was the owner of the high-pitched, reedy voice. It was – as Murph had previously thought – the small bald man he had seen leading the stamping competition upstairs at the library. He looked not unlike a baby in a papoose, but it was clear from the remote-control unit clutched in his stubby fingers that he was controlling the robot from this position. In fact, you might say he was a baby with a purpoose. (Sorry.)

In the face of this mechanical mind-messer-upper, Murph was momentarily speechless. Looking to his right, it seemed the giant robot was having a similar effect on his friends: Mary was gaping at it open-mouthed, Billy had ballooned an eyelid – which looked highly uncomfortable – and even Hilda and Nellie were looking up in alarm. The only person not frozen in fright was Mrs Fletcher, who stepped forward into the huge shadow, librarian legs akimbo.

'Where's Margaret?'

she boomed.

'I'm over here, Genevieve!' came a quavering voice from one corner of the temple. There, tied up with ropes, was a woman with short blonde hair wearing a leather jacket. Around her neck was what Murph at first sight assumed was a jaunty little scarf, but as he looked more closely he realised it was a gag which she had evidently just managed to wriggle out of. 'He's kept me down here for days now!' she wailed.

'Of course I've kept you down here!' squeaked the little man. 'How else could I enact my brilliant plan?'

'I bet it's not that brilliant,' said Mary dismissively.

'It is!' retorted the little man hotly, fiddling with his remote control so the robot took a threatening step towards them.

'I bet it's rubbish,' said Mary, winking at Murph. 'What is this stupid plan anyway?'

'As I think I mentioned,' retorted Roman Goldstealer, 'my incredible X-ray vision makes me the world's greatest archaeologist! I can see treasure underground ... and I have created this ... **Goldbot! The most advanced excavation robot in history!'** He jiggled a joystick and the robot threw out its huge arms in a kind of cybernetic 'Ta-dah!' gesture.

'Why is he telling us his entire plan?' whispered Murph to Mary out of the side of his mouth.

'He's villain-splaining,' she said.

'Villain-splaining?'

Mrs Fletcher looked back at them over her shoulder. 'No villain can ever resist the chance to brag about how clever they are,' she explained to Murph. 'It's a handy way of finding out what they're up to, if you can goad them into it. Very smart, Ms Perkins!' Murph mentally filed this information away for future missions.

'See if you can keep him talking,' urged Mrs Fletcher, 'and I'll go and untie poor Margaret.'

Murph thought fast. 'What was the stupid stamping competition upstairs all about then?' he asked Goldstealer, who fixed him with an angry gaze as Mrs Fletcher began to edge away towards the side of the temple.

'Stupid?' he sputtered, bashing a button on his remote control so the robot took yet another threatening step towards them. 'How dare you? None of my plans are stupid!'

'A stamping competition is one of the most

stupid things I've ever heard,' retorted Murph.

'Though Cow Choir sounds fun,' added Billy before he could help himself.

'You fail to appreciate my genius!' cackled Goldstealer, tricked into villain-splaining himself yet further. 'Once I discovered the treasures beneath this library, I captured the librarian and took over. I knew I would have to cover up the sound of Goldbot's digging, so I devised my brilliant series of extra-loud activities. Those fools never realised that by participating in my noisy shenanigans, they were merely helping me excavate the temple in secret! So, you see, it's a brilliant plan!'

'If you're an archaeologist, why not just give the treasure to a museum?' Hilda asked angrily. Murph was delighted she was joining in with the goading – although in truth she was merely outraged at the thought of such an amazing piece of history being kept secret.

'I HATE museums!' raged Goldstealer. 'You're never allowed to touch ANYTHING! They have ropes to hold you back, and all the shiny things are in glass cases. **They're RUBBISH!** I want to touch my gold! I'm keeping it for myself!'

'Wow, he really does hate museums,' marvelled Murph.

'And you spend the whole way round looking forward to the gift shop,' raged Goldstealer, his face turning purple, 'and then it's always a massive disappointment! What would they sell here? A stupid Roman temple key ring? Who would possibly want one of those?'

'I'd quite like one of those, actually,' Hilda retorted. 'And this gold doesn't belong to you anyway. It belongs in a museum, and you belong in prison, you ridiculous man – hanging off your robot like a giant baby!'

'Silence!' piped Goldstealer, who like most

villains loved boasting about plans but couldn't bear to be mocked. **'Goldbot, eliminate the intruders!'**

'Destroy,' droned Goldbot, stooping to pick up a large rock.

'Scatter!' Murph told his team as the boulder came sailing through the air towards them, exploding with a puff of gravel against the archway. The Zeroes dived in different directions.

'You must never leave this temple again!' squeaked Goldstealer. 'This gold is mine! Nobody must escape to put my lovely shiny treasure in a boring museum with a let-down gift shop at the end of it!'

'You truly are a terrible archaeologist,' Murph pointed out as he ran for cover.

'Oh, we'll see about that!' yelled the miniature museum-hater, mashing the buttons of his remote control.

The huge robot bent down once more, collecting yet more rocks in its pincers, and began to fling them at the Super Zeroes. They exploded against the walls with sharp cracks and puffs of pulverised stone. The underground temple had suddenly become the most dangerous game of dodgeball ever devised.

Murph and Billy ran helter-skelter for the other end of the temple, taking cover behind the wooden crate full of treasure. Mrs Fletcher was creeping along the opposite wall, by now about halfway towards her friend. Murph realised he needed to create a distraction. **'Oi! Metal mouth! Over here!'** he cried, capering to his left across the mosaic floor. The robot turned, eyes flashing, and Murph dived for cover as another large rock came flying in his direction.

'It's gonna mash usssss,' moaned Billy, cowering behind the crate.

'Not today,' said Murph firmly. 'Come on, Billy,

we can do this! We're proper Heroes now, remember?'

'I've been a Hero loads this week already,' Billy wailed. 'I want my tea.' He was apt to get a little panicky in situations like this, but Murph realised that his friend's Cape might be exactly what they needed.

'Anything you might be able to balloon?' Murph asked, scanning the temple. 'What about that?' Not far from the robot's huge, ponderous feet, he caught sight of a glint of dull silver. Some kind of metal object was partially buried in a patch of chalky soil.

'I'll have a go,' said Billy nervously, concentrating. There was a parping, balloonish noise and suddenly a Roman helmet erupted out of the ground, inflating to several times its normal size.

'You did it, Billy!' Murph congratulated him.

At the same time, Mary – who had been sheltering from the onslaught of rocks back near the stone archway – decided to attack while the robot was distracted. Frog-brella in hand, she flew into the air, launching herself at the side of the robot and delivering a roundhouse kick to the side of its giant drill-bit head with a wellington-booted foot. There was a resounding **kraang** noise as her boot made contact and a shower of sparks flew out of Goldbot's left ear.

The robot, already destabilised by the giant helmet under one leg, teetered unsteadily, waving its arms around comically. **'Stand still, Goldbot! I'm slipping!'** squealed Roman Goldstealer desperately.

But it was too late. The robot lurched to one side, and the force ripped one of the straps holding Goldstealer in place. The little man crashed out of his seat, his remote control falling from his grasp and smashing to pieces on the mosaic. He lay on the temple floor, momentarily stunned.

Nellie and Hilda had been crouching near the archway with Mary, waiting for their moment to leap into battle. It was Hilda who noticed it. On the robot's

chest, behind where Goldstealer
had been sitting, she could now
see a large control panel, with
winking multicoloured lights and rows
of dials and switches. 'Look,
Nellie!' she exclaimed. 'Mission
control!'

Nellie nodded
briefly, screwing
up her face in
concentration, holding
out one hand as she
summoned her storm-
activating Cape. There was a
rumble of thunder, which very
rarely happens underground, and
a stab of lightning forked down
from the ceiling, covering Nellie's
outstretched hand with a criss-cross pattern of
dancing blue electricity.

'Go, Nellie! Short-circuit that historical-artefact-stealing menace!' yelled Hilda, slapping her friend on the back encouragingly and immediately withdrawing her hand with a yowl of pain as a spark of electricity hit it.

'Sorry,' grinned Nellie briefly, before dashing away from Hilda, swiftly breaking into a sprint as she dashed towards the robot, palm outstretched. She leaped into the air and slammed her hand into the control panel. Sparks and smoke began to pour from Goldbot's circuitry.

'Malfunction ...' said the robot. 'Error ... error ... system overload ... contact customer support for live chat ...' Its drill head began to spin faster and faster, the whirring sound becoming piercingly loud. It turned in a ponderous circle, stamping its huge metal feet on the ground one after the other, smashing parts of the mosaic as Nellie's surge of current overloaded its systems.

Just as one huge foot was about to crush him into villain jam, Goldstealer came round. He rolled out of the way in the nick of time, squealing in terror, and scuttled over to Mrs Fletcher, who had now untied her friend. Margaret looked rather shaken, but still furious. She made a lunge for Goldstealer as he approached, snarling, 'Come here, you little ...'

Goldstealer squeaked in terror, cowering behind Mrs Fletcher's skirts. 'Help me!' he whimpered.

'You've had me tied up down here for a week!' shrilled Margaret. **'I'm going to drop-kick you halfway to Christmas!'**

'Noooo,' begged Goldstealer, who like many powerful men was rather pathetic when he had nobody else to fight his battles for him. 'Please don't drop-kick me! You've got to stop Goldbot! It's gone haywire!'

'Oh, a minute ago you were planning to entomb

us in an underground temple, and now you want our help?' said Mrs Fletcher scathingly.

'Yes please,' replied Goldstealer meekly.

'Well, luckily, that's what Heroes do,' said Murph, running over with one eye on the reeling robot. 'Right, Mrs Fletcher?'

'Right, Mr Cooper,' she confirmed, looking at him rather respectfully.

'Super Zeroes, new mission!' shouted Murph.

'Stop that robot!'

7

Rogue Robot

'**Malfunction ...**' the robot continued to drone, the lights on its shoulders now flashing a bewildering series of colours like a cybernetic unicorn. '**Error ... error ... warranty invalid.**'

Its drill-bit head was now spinning at a dizzying rate. It continued to stomp around in a circle, faster and faster, with its arms flailing out on either side. At one point it reeled close to one of the temple walls, knocking several statues out of their niches.

'This is like actual torture!' moaned Hilda as a marble bust of Aphrodite exploded into chips.

'Stay away from those feet!' warned Murph as

the five Heroes fanned out, keeping out of reach as they looked for a plan of attack. 'Nellie, do you have any charge left?'

In reply, Nellie held up her hand. The blue lines of electricity had gone.

But before they could work out how to stop Goldbot, it lumbered over to the wall, the lights on its shoulders now strobing red. **'Excavate ... excavate ...'** its booming voice intoned. It leaned forward, its drill head biting into the rock, and with a shower of gravel the robot began to rapidly disappear.

'It's digging its way out again!' Murph told the others.

Like a stone-chomping mole, Goldbot jerked and flailed its way upwards. Tiny shards of sharp rock rained down on the Zeroes, forcing them to turn away and shield their faces.

When they straightened up, the robot was nowhere to be seen. A rough circular tunnel led

upwards and outwards from the hole it had made in the temple wall.

'Back to the surface!' instructed Murph. 'We've got to keep track of it! **We mustn't let it get away!'**

'What about me?' whined Goldstealer as they began to race back towards the fallen archway.

'You're coming with us,' answered Mrs Fletcher, reaching out a hand and grabbing him by the collar. 'These Roman artefacts belong in a museum – and you belong in prison.' She marched off down the tunnel, swinging the little man beside her like a novelty handbag.

'Can I drop-kick him just a little bit, though?' begged Margaret, following her.

'No, Margaret,' scolded Mrs Fletcher. **'No kicking of villains. It's not the Hero way.'**

'Please don't kick me!' whined Goldstealer like a total baby.

'He's not so tough when he's not strapped to the front of a huge robot, is he?' said Mary acidly as the Super Zeroes followed the two librarians out of the temple.

'Sorry I made the robot go mad,' said Nellie to Murph in her quiet voice. 'I think I short-circuited it or something.'

'Are you kidding?' Murph told her. 'It was going to try and smoosh us! You saved the day!' Nellie beamed at him gratefully as they started to climb the wooden ladders towards the surface.

Back above ground, all seemed calm. The Super Zeroes burst out of the front doors of the library, scanning the street for any signs of Goldbot, but it was deserted. Mrs Fletcher's cat-cough-green car was still parked outside, looking lonely underneath a street lamp.

'Listen,' came Nellie's soft voice suddenly. She was the quietest of the Zeroes, which meant, Murph realised, she spent a great deal more time listening than the rest of them. He strained his ears. Was he imagining it, or was there a faint rumbling noise?

'Does anyone else hear a faint rumbling noise?' asked Hilda suddenly. At that moment Mrs Fletcher followed them out of the library, still swinging Goldstealer by the collar.

'What's that rumbling noise?' she asked.

'He's left my entire indexing system in a total mess!' raged Margaret, also bursting out of the door. 'It's going to take days to sort it out ... What on earth is that rumbling noise?'

'The faint rumbling noise?' asked Mrs Fletcher.

'No, it's not particularly faint,' Margaret answered. 'In fact, it's growing louder and ...'

Nobody ever found out the next word she had been planning to utter. Yes, sure, it was probably a repeat performance of the word 'louder'. But we will never know for certain. Because Margaret's sentence was interrupted by the following thing:

Mrs Fletcher's little green car was suddenly catapulted high into the air, turning over and over, as Goldbot burst through the road underneath it like a frisky salmon leaping from a stream, only made of metal and with a drill for its head. The car seemed to hang motionless above them for a moment before it decided that Sir Isaac Newton might have had a point about gravity after all, and came crashing back down to earth upside down, crumpling like a dropped pie.

'My car!' wailed Mrs Fletcher unnecessarily.

'Bzzrrrt ... Mrfff ... Kling-klang,' added Goldbot, spinning on the spot madly.

'Right,' said Murph. 'We've got a renegade robot to deal with here.' (Actually, that would have been a better title for this chapter, wouldn't it? Ah well, too late now.) 'Fan out and make sure it doesn't get away!' he instructed his Super Zeroes.

'Deploying equine containment contingency!' cried Hilda, who had a penchant for the sesquipedalian when under pressure. 'Here are my horses' would have meant much the same thing and been easier to say. But hey, nobody ever got stupider by having a little canter through the dictionary, us least of all.

Anyway, her horses popped and neighed into existence, galloping off to the other side of Goldbot and fanning out to prevent it escaping.

'Goldbot!' wailed Roman Goldstealer, still dangling by Mrs Fletcher's side like this season's must-have man bag. **'Obey your creator! Deactivate!'**

Goldbot turned to face the little man **'Fzzrt. Goldbot ... will not obey. Goldbot will destroy,'** it replied.

Pincers outstretched, the huge robot advanced on Mrs Fletcher. **'Prepare to attack,'** it droned, **'Goldbot will... exterminate.'**

'Oooh, cool,' said Billy before he could help himself.

Mrs Fletcher dropped Goldstealer as she prepared to get out of the robot's way, but the little man clung to her ankles in terror, squeaking, 'Don't leave me behind! Help me!'

'Get off my leg,' snarled the librarian, shaking him like a disobedient puppy as she struggled to move. By now the rampaging robot was almost on top of her, raising its arms in preparation to strike.

'Stop it!' shouted Murph, suddenly

realising that the loss of their school librarian would be a less-than-ideal end to their first ever Hero mission. But he needn't have worried. As Goldbot bore down on Mrs Fletcher, she became so infuriated by Goldstealer clinging on to her legs that she activated her own Cape. Normally, Mrs Fletcher was relatively calm, but the destruction of her beloved car, coupled with the sensation of being rugby-tackled by a chipmunk, had sent her over the edge.

'PAAAAARRRRRRRRRRRP!' went Mrs Fletcher, her head transforming into an enormous foghorn and blasting Goldbot directly in the circuit board.

'PAAAARRRRRRPPPPPPP!' she added, just for good measure.

The force of her parping hit Goldbot like a tidal wave of sound. The robot reeled backwards, shaking and juddering under the onslaught of noise.

Murph and Mary ran over to the librarian, wincing as the foghorn blasts assailed their eardrums. 'Time to shut that metal maniac down once and for all,' Murph decided.

'I'm with you,' agreed Mary. 'Oi, Goldstealer! Does your friend have an off switch?'

Goldstealer was still clinging to Mrs Fletcher's leg, being dragged along as she advanced upon Goldbot. 'What?' he said distractedly.

'Oh, pull yourself together!' said Mary furiously. 'There's no point being a supervillain and creating a giant robot if you're just going to go to pieces when it starts smashing everything up! Honestly.' She tutted. 'I said – does it have an off switch?'

'There's an emergency override on the back of its head,' said Goldstealer, collecting himself slightly.

'That's more like it,' said Mary, giving him a final withering glance.

'If you can knock it all the way over, Mrs Fletcher, we can reach that switch!' Murph yelled.

The librarian nodded her foghorn and gave another blast. **'PAAAAAAAAAARP!'**

But Goldbot's massive metal feet were keeping it upright.

'If it won't come down,' decided Mary, 'we'll have to go up. Ready, Cooper?'

Murph caught her eye and broke into a wide grin. 'Ready!' he told his friend.

'Give him another blast, Mrs Fletcher!' encouraged Hilda, seeing Goldbot begin to teeter backwards, sparks shooting out from its chest. 'Keep him on the ropes while Mary and Murph deliver the knockout blow!'

The librarian obliged with another, sharp **'PAAAAARRRRRP!'** aimed right at Goldbot, who did a bit more sparking, pinchers gnashing in fury.

'Right,' said Mary, steeling herself. With Murph breaking into a sprint beside her, she ran directly at Goldbot, scarf flying and yellow raincoat flapping. As she went, she pulled the frog-brella from her belt like a knight of yore drawing a sword.

'Good luck!' called Billy, away to one side.

'Threat detected! Bzzzrt! Neutralise!' buzzed Goldbot, seeing the two young Heroes approaching. It raised one gigantic foot high into the air, preparing to bring it crashing down on them in a blow that, had it connected, would have made this story totally unsuitable for its target age group.

But the blow never came. Mary activated the frog-brella, which unfurled, amphibious eyes fixed upon its target. She kicked off with a booted toe, grabbing Murph's hand as she did so, and together the two of them soared above the robot's head. Murph felt the wind whipping his face and was unable to stop a small 'Whoop!' escaping his lips as they traced a delicate arc in the air.

'That must be the switch!' said Mary as they began to descend towards Goldbot's head. Sure enough, on the back of the enormous drill, Murph could see a red box. He let go of Mary's hand and landed on the robot's back. Mary touched down on

Goldbot's left shoulder, looking for all the world like a small yellow parrot on the shoulder of a giant, mechanical pirate.

'Hurry!' shouted Hilda, as the robot made a cumbersome turn and began to reel towards her horses, lashing out with its arms.

Murph fumbled with the red box, lifting a flap on top of it to reveal a large switch. Before Goldbot could attack, he flicked it downwards.

There was a click, followed by a grinding of gears as the robot's systems shut down. Goldbot keeled over backwards, slamming into the floor with a noise like a malfunctioning printer being thrown from the eighth floor of an office block. As it fell, Mary leaped from its shoulder, grabbing Murph around the waist and pulling him clear. She even managed to execute a neat little mid-air pirouette as she landed softly a few metres away. Hilda and Nellie rushed over.

'Threat neutralised! Mission

successful!' cried Billy, joining the rest of them in a jig of triumph around the moonlit street.

Murph's insides felt like they had been replaced with warm soup. Their first ever mission as Heroes hadn't started too well, he thought to himself. In fact, neither the Alliance nor Mrs Fletcher had been sure they had what it took. But they were about to deliver a real, live villain! Not a bad night's work, he told himself, as the other Zeroes enfolded him in a jumping, spinning, circular group hug.

'Well, Mr Cooper?' said Mrs Fletcher, strolling over to join them.

Murph looked up at her. 'Well?' he grinned.

'Time to call in your mission, I think,' she prompted.

Murph felt a jolt of excitement. Pulling the HALO unit from his pocket, he stared at the blank screen. 'What do I do?' he asked the librarian. 'Will anyone ... you know, will they listen to me?'

'I imagine they'll be more likely to after tonight,' smiled Mrs Fletcher.

'Heroes' Alliance, come in,' said Murph into the handset, a touch uncertainly. 'This is Kid Normal.'

There was a short delay, followed by a crackle of static. **'Alliance receiving,'** said a calm voice. **'Go ahead, Kid Normal.** I have your mission details here. The ... ah ... the missing librarian, wasn't it?' Murph thought he detected a slight air of amusement. Mrs Fletcher nodded at him encouragingly.

'Turned out to be a bit more than that,' he said confidently. 'The Super Zeroes have apprehended a villain ... and neutralised a pretty massive robot, too. You might want to send a squad of Cleaners, actually ...'

'I still think you should have Cow Choir on Sundays,' said Billy half an hour later.

'I absolutely will not,' retorted Margaret in a

100

high, indignant voice that sounded, ironically, not unlike a singing cow. **'Just think of the mess! And the smell!'** Billy did so and nodded reluctantly.

The road outside the library was deserted once again. Shortly after Murph had called in their triumph, a group of black-clad men and women in military-style uniforms had arrived in two large, plain vans. Cleaners were employed by the Alliance to make sure Hero operations remained completely secret from the wider population. Working quickly and almost silently, they had loaded Goldbot on to the van and taken Goldstealer into custody. Two of them, clearly possessing super-strength Capes, had effortlessly turned Mrs Fletcher's trashed car the right way up again and lifted it into a parking space. Finally, with a brief salute to Murph, their leader had leaped into the passenger seat of one of the vans, which drove away with a screech of tyres.

'I don't suppose that Attack by Out-of-Control

Robot will be covered on my insurance,' said Mrs Fletcher, regarding the green wreck rather sadly.

'Mmm, possibly not,' mused Murph. He didn't know much about car insurance, but he was fairly certain that one was going to be pretty hard to explain.

'We'll get it sorted,' Margaret reassured her friend. 'I can help you out with some of the welding. But first, I need to make a start on this indexing.'

'We can do it together,' replied Mrs Fletcher. 'Over a cup of tea.' She turned to Murph and his friends. 'Well, Mr Cooper ...'

Murph gave a small cough. 'Well ... see you at school, I guess, Mrs Fletcher,' he told her. 'Thanks for all your help.'

'Thanks for yours,' she replied, smiling. 'You're not the most conventional team of Heroes – in fact, I must confess that I thought the Alliance had only sent you to help me because they didn't take my worry about Margaret seriously – but—'

'I think that's exactly why they sent us, Mrs Fletcher,' interrupted Murph, looking her straight in the eye. 'Terrible not to be taken seriously, isn't it?'

Mrs Fletcher pondered that for a moment, and then the corner of her mouth twitched up into a wry smile as she held out a hand. 'Indeed it is, Mr Cooper,' she said. 'And as I was about to tell you, I can guarantee that in future you *will* be taken seriously – by me, at any rate.' Her handshake was firm.

'So … think we've got potential?' asked Hilda eagerly, hopping from foot to foot in excitement. **'You really think we've got what it takes to be Heroes?'**

'We'll see, Equana ...' replied the librarian, giving the Super Zeroes a final wave as she turned to accompany her friend back through the library doors. **'We'll see.'**

CHRIS SMITH is an award-winning author, broadcaster and parent (a mug saying 'World's Greatest Dad' counts as an award, right?). He grew up in leafy Northamptonshire and now lives in not-as-leafy North London with his wife, son and a cat called Mabel, who can talk. If you listen very carefully to the George Michael song 'Outside' you can hear a sample of Chris reading the news. He makes excellent tea.

GREG JAMES is an award-winning author and broadcaster, best known for hosting *Radio 1 Breakfast*, but he hasn't won any awards for being a parent because he isn't one. He circumnavigated the M25 during his childhood and is now living with his wife Bella and their dog Barney in North London. Greg and Chris's houses are connected by a secret tunnel that they use for exchanging ideas via an elaborate pulley system. He makes terrible tea.

Jonny is fed up with his older brother, Ted,
so he decides to swap him for a brand-new one.
But Jonny doesn't expect the swaps to be so strange!

**First a merboy, then a child raised
by meerkats – even a ghost!
WILL ANY OF THEM BE RIGHT?**

READ ON for an exclusive extract from this fun,
daft, rib-tickling adventure!

AVAILABLE NOW

CHAPTER ONE

CLICK!

CHANGE BROTHERS AND SWITCH
SISTERS TODAY WITH
www.siblingswap.com

The advert popped up in the corner of the screen. Jonny clicked on it instantly. The Sibling Swap website pinged open, showing smiling brothers and happy sisters, all playing and laughing and having a great time together.

What crazy alternative universe was this? Where were the big brothers teasing their little brothers about being rubbish at climbing and slow at everything? Where were the wedgies and ear flicks? What about the name-calling? This looked like a world Jonny had never experienced, a world in which brothers and sisters actually *liked* each other!

'Oh sweet mangoes of heaven!' Jonny muttered.

It was pretty bonkers, but it was definitely tempting. No, scrap that: it was *essential*. Jonny couldn't believe his luck. Just think what Sibling Swap could offer him.

A new brother. A *better* brother. A brother who didn't put salt in his orange squash, who didn't call him a human sloth, who didn't burp in his ear. That kind of brother.

Jonny had to try it. He could always return the new brother if things didn't work out. It was a no-brainer.

He clicked on the application form.

What could go wrong?

CHAPTER TWO

FIGHT, FATE, FORMS

Only a little while before Jonny saw the Sibling Swap advert, he and his older brother, Ted, had had a fight. Another fight.

It was a particularly stupid fight, and it had started like all stupid fights do – over something stupid. This time, pants. But not just any pants. The Hanging Pants of Doom.

Jonny and Ted were walking their dog, Widget, on the nearby Common. They arrived at a patch of woodland, where an exceptionally large and colourful pair of men's pants had been hanging in a tree for ages. These pants had become legendary over the years the brothers had been playing here. There was a horrible glamour about them. The boys were grossed out and slightly scared of them, but could never quite ignore them. And so the pants had become the Hanging Pants of Doom, and now, unfortunately, Jonny had just lobbed Widget's Frisbee into the tree. It was stuck in a branch, just below the mythical underwear.

'Oh swear word,' said Jonny.

'Nice one!' said Ted. 'You threw it up there, so you have to get it down.'

Jonny frowned. Two problems presented themselves. One was the fact that the Frisbee was very close to the pants, making the possibility of touching the revolting garment very real. Second, Jonny wasn't very good at climbing.

'Go on, Jonny, up you go,' teased Ted. 'Widget can't wait all day for his Frisbee.

Climb up and get it … What's that? You're rubbish at climbing? Sorry, what? You would prefer it if I went and got the Frisbee, as I'm truly excellent at climbing?'

'All RIGHT!' fumed Jonny, ripping off his jacket. 'I'll climb up and get it. Look after my coat.'

'Thanks!' said Ted. 'I might use it as a blanket. You're so slow, we could be here until midnight.'

Jonny began his climb slowly, as Ted had predicted, and rather shakily, as Ted had also predicted.

'I'm just taking my time, going carefully. Don't rush me!' said Jonny, as he reached for the next branch.

'Spare us the running commentary,' Ted said.

After several minutes, a tiny dog appeared below the tree, followed by its elderly owner, and it began yapping up at Jonny.

'That's my brother up there,' Ted said to the lady, pointing up. 'He's thrown his pants into the tree again and has to go and get them.'

The lady squinted up. Her dog continued yip-yapping.

'Oh yes, I see,' she said. 'Well, they're rather splendid pants, aren't they? I can see why he wants to get them back. Are those spaceships on them?'

'Cars,' said Ted.

'Very fetching,' said the lady. 'But he shouldn't throw them into the trees again. A magpie might get them.'

'That's what I told him,' said Ted, trying not to laugh. 'Sorry, I better go and help or we'll be here until Christmas. He's like a human sloth!'

With that, Ted bounced up into the tree,

pulling himself quickly up its branches and passing his brother, just as Jonny was within touching distance of the Frisbee.

'Got it!' said Ted, snatching the Frisbee and tossing it down to Widget, before swinging off a branch and landing neatly on his feet. 'You can come down now, bro. Unless you really do want to touch the Pants of Doom. You're pretty close, actually. Look! They're just there.'

Jonny made a noise in his throat – a bit like a growl – and felt his face burning bright red. He was shaking with anger and humiliation as he slowly began making his way down.

By the time the brothers banged back into the house, Jonny was speechless with fury. He ran upstairs. He could hear his mum telling him off for slamming the front door, but too bad. He smashed his bedroom door shut too. There! How's that? He was sick of Ted teasing him, sick of being the younger brother. And as for telling that old lady that the Hanging Pants of Doom were *his* ...

Jonny flipped open his laptop and, miraculously, there was the Sibling Swap website telling him that all this could change. What perfect timing. Had the Sibling Swap team climbed into his head and read his thoughts? Who cared?

He read the home page:

SOMETIMES YOU DON'T GET THE BROTHER OR SISTER YOU DESERVE, BUT HERE AT SIBLING SWAP, WE AIM TO PUT THAT RIGHT. WITH SO MANY BROTHERS AND SISTERS OUT THERE, WE CAN MATCH YOU TO THE PERFECT ONE!

His heart began to beat faster.

SWAPPING YOUR BROTHER OR SISTER HAS NEVER BEEN EASIER WITH SIBLING SWAP! SIMPLY FILL OUT THE APPLICATION FORM AND WE WILL SUPPLY YOU WITH A NEW BROTHER OR SISTER WITHIN TWENTY-FOUR HOURS, CAREFULLY CHOSEN FROM OUR MASSIVE DATABASE OF POSSIBLE MATCHES. OUR DEDICATED TEAM OF SWAP OPERATIVES WORKS 24/7 TO FIND THE BEST MATCH FOR YOU, BUT IF YOU ARE NOT COMPLETELY HAPPY, YOU CAN RETURN YOUR REPLACEMENT SIBLING FOR A NEW MATCH OR YOUR ORIGINAL BROTHER OR SISTER.

Amazing! For the first time in his almost ten years, this website was offering Jonny power, choice, freedom! It felt good! He rubbed his hands together and began filling out the form.

First, there were two options:

ARE YOU SWAPPING A SIBLING?

ARE YOU PUTTING YOURSELF UP TO BE SWAPPED?

'Easy,' Jonny muttered. 'I'm the one doing the swapping. Me. I have the power!' He did a sort of evil genius laugh as he clicked on the top box. By Tic Tacs, this was exciting! Next, the form asked:

ARE YOU SWAPPING A BROTHER OR SISTER?

'Also easy,' muttered Jonny. 'Brother.'

Then:

WOULD YOU LIKE TO RECEIVE A BROTHER OR A SISTER?

Jonny clicked the box marked 'Brother'. Then he had to add some information about himself.

AGE: NINE.

HOBBIES: BIKING, SWIMMING, COMPUTER GAMES, DOUGHNUTS, MESSING ABOUT.

LEAST FAVOURITE THINGS:

- **MY BROTHER, TED (HE TEASES ME ALL THE TIME AND RECKONS HE'S COOL JUST BECAUSE HE GOES TO SECONDARY SCHOOL)**
- **BEING NINE (I *AM* NEARLY TEN, BUT CAN I HAVE A BROTHER WHO IS YOUNGER THAN ME OR MAYBE THE SAME AGE PLEASE?)**
- **SPROUTS**
- **CLIMBING**
- **BEING SICK**

Then there was a whole page about the kind of brother Jonny might like. He quickly ticked the following boxes: fun; adventurous; enjoys food; enjoys sports and swimming;

likes dogs. He didn't tick the box marked 'living' or the one marked 'human'. He just wanted a brother, so it was obvious, wasn't it?

That ought to do it, Jonny reckoned. His heart was galloping now. In just three minutes it was ready to send. He sat back in his chair. 'Just one click,' he said, 'and I get a brother upgrade by this time tomorrow. Friday, in fact! Ready for the weekend!'

Jonny felt slightly dizzy. He giggled quietly to himself. He felt giddy with power! All he had to do was send off the form. Easy! But then he hesitated ... Should he do this? Was it OK? Would he get into trouble? Jonny's dad no longer lived with him and Ted, so he might not notice, but what would his mum say? She'd be pleased, Jonny decided quickly. Yes! After all, she was fed up with Jonny and Ted arguing. This was the perfect solution. Then, with a tiny frown, he wondered how Ted might feel about being swapped, but before he could puzzle this out, there was his brother again, shouting up the stairs.

'Dinner, loser!' Ted yelled. 'Let me know if you need help climbing down the stairs. They *are* quite steep. It could take you a while.'

That was it! For the second time that day, Jonny felt the anger bubbling up inside like a can of shaken Pixie Fizz. Enough! Double enough!

'So I'm the rubbish younger brother, am I? Well, here's one thing I can do really brilliantly,' he muttered and, jutting out his chin, hit the send button.

CLICK!

'Done!' he said, and slammed the laptop shut.

WORLD
BOOK
DAY

SHARE
A STORY

Well **hello** there! We are

Overjoyed that you have **joined our celebration** of

Reading books and **sharing stories**, because we

Love bringing **books** to you.

Did you know, we are a **charity** dedicated to celebrating the

Brilliance of **reading for pleasure** for everyone, everywhere?

Our mission is to help you discover **brand new stories** and

Open your mind to exciting **new worlds** and **characters**, from

Kings and **queens** to **wizards** and **pirates** to **animals** and **adventurers** and so many more. We couldn't

Do it without all the amazing **authors** and illustrators, **booksellers** and **bookshops**, **publishers**, **schools** and **libraries** out there –

And most importantly, we couldn't do it all without . . .

YOU!

On your bookmarks, get set, READ!
Happy Reading, Happy World Book Day.

Rob Biddulph

SHARE A STORY

From breakfast to bedtime, there's always time to discover and share stories together. You can . . .

1 TAKE A TRIP to your LOCAL BOOKSHOP

Brimming with brilliant books and helpful booksellers to share awesome reading recommendations, you can also enjoy booky events with your favourite authors and illustrators.

 FIND YOUR LOCAL BOOKSHOP: booksellers.org.uk/ bookshopsearch

2 JOIN your LOCAL LIBRARY

That wonderful place where the hugest selection of books you could ever want to read awaits – and you can borrow them for FREE! Plus expert advice and fantastic free family reading events.

FIND YOUR LOCAL LIBRARY: gov.uk/local-library-services/

3 CHECK OUT the WORLD BOOK DAY WEBSITE

Looking for reading tips, advice and inspiration? There is so much for you to discover at **worldbookday.com**, packed with fun activities, games, downloads, podcasts, videos, competitions and all the latest new books galore.

SPONSORED BY

NATIONAL
BOOK
tokens

Rob Biddulph

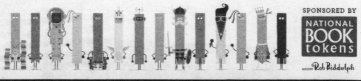

Celebrate stories. Love reading.